CODY GOODFELLOW
IN PRAISE OF SEX
& VIOLENCE
2-5

UNKLE KRUST'S GUIDE TO
FEMALE LADY-TYPE WOMEN
6-7

GREGORY BOSSERT
THE DAMSEL OF DESIRE
8-17

MICHAEL ALLEN ROSE
INCUBUS SUCCUBUS
IAMBUS*
18-21

JEFF STRAND
GREEN SUITS
22-25

MIKE DUBISCH
CHICKEN OR FISH
26-27

CRAIG LAURANCE GIDNEY
(K)NAIVETY
28-29

EDWARD LEE
THE STATEMENT OF
SGT JUSTIN JESSOP OF
THE INNSMOUTH
POLICE DEPARTMENT
31-33

BRENDAN VIDITO
MOTHER'S MARK*
34-35

MATTHEW BARTLETT
THE KING-HOLE CHRONICLES
VOL. 8 INSTALLMENT 2:
THE NEW KING
36-41

KIM VODICKA
PLASTER CASTER
42-43

ED KURTZ
THE IMP AND THE
SMOKE ANGEL
44-45

CREDITS
ARTIST & AUTHORS
46-47

publisher: ODDNESS
artwork: MIKE DUBISCH
editor: CODY GOODFELLOW
colorist: CAROYLN DUBISCH WATSON*

FORBIDDEN FUTURES 7

ISBN: 9781960213129 (v1.5):

FORBIDDEN FUTURES 7

IN PRAISE OF SEX & VIOLENCE
BY CODY GOODFELLOW

"Yippee Kay-Aye, Mister Falcon..."
—Bruce Willis, *Die Hard* (edited for broadcast television)

It's a hoary cliche in American cultural criticism that if you kiss a breast in a story or film, you'll get in a lot more trouble than if you stab one. Of course, despite the censors' best efforts to preserve our childlike innocence, anyone who can work a computer can instantly see almost literally anything, but how has our continued hypocrisy towards sex and violence deformed artistic depictions of both?

While we can finally have everything we ever thought we wanted, everything has become porn—an empty, self-justifying indulgence sanitized of truth or consequences until it has as much in common with real human interaction as kabuki. Even in the edgiest content on offer, sex still causes problems that only violence can solve.

While many of us who grew up under the iron fists of broadcast standards & practices, the Million Moms and the MPAA revel in this new era of sleazy glasnost, what is and isn't acceptable in mainstream culture has become a political football in the culture wars. Outrage for its own sake has too much tactical value to be weakened by precedent or objective standards of morality or taste. Witness the chronic moral crises of video-game violence as a red herring lobbed into every mass shooting tragedy, or the Super Bowl Halftime Show being perennially rebuked by scandalized folks who have no problem with a self-professed sexual predator in the White House. *The Purge* franchise and *The Hunt* reaped cheap outrage not for their overkill, but for *who* gets killed, as cultural conservatives get ever more triggered by depictions of the civil war they've been loudly spoiling for.

They can't stop us from bingeing all we want and in this quarantine, it's pretty much our only job—so we have only the market and ourselves to blame for all the nostalgic gore and action porn we're getting.

In an age of cheap and easy digital bloodspray, the lost art of practical fx persists as a retro synthcore trip to Reaganaut days when heads popped like champagne corks off boneless bodies filled with homogenous corn syrup goo. But in slavishly paying homage to the golden age of gore, what's left out is any of the thematic marrow that made those original films memorable. Icons like Carpenter and Cronenberg built on their influences and understood that shocking visuals needed equally shocking ideas. Any genre becomes a museum piece when it settles into being a genre of things—of familiar premises, themes and aesthetics. Even the most confrontational art becomes comfort food when we know what to expect. (By this metric, three of the best horror movies in recent years are from outside the genre—*Funny Games, Green Room* and *Let The Corpses Tan* beautifully tear down the most rancid cliches about just how much abuse the human mind and body can withstand, and are damn good horror, to boot.)

The current state of the action genre seems like weird mission creep from the jingoistic propaganda we grew up on in the 80's. Now that military recruitment leans so heavily on economic hardship and immigrant aspirations, with the bulk of the public completely insulated from the hardships of service, it's decoupled from patriotic themes to drift into full-on revenge and grievance fantasies, telling dangerously stupid lies about the nature of violence itself.

Stallone's immortal roid-rage golem *Rambo* shambles on to unwittingly point out every outdated delusion we still entertain about the nature of American power, but it's a straight docudrama next to his *Expendables* trilogy, which turns war into an apolitical, PTSD-free fantasy stunt-show... seriously, if they're expendable, why are there MORE of them laughing even harder at the end of every installment, and none of them ever gets killed?

You can convince every sheep in the fold that they're secretly a wolf with hyper-stylized red-placebo ultraviolence like the *John Wick* franchise, whose choreographed gun-fu extravaganzas turn death into a dance competition. And in the name of demographic outreach, there's the whole sub-genre of *La Femme Nikita* knockoffs, with eerily beautiful nymphets turning on the patriarchy that made them into grrl-powered killing machines. It's like they asked the Mountain Dew-chugging AI that generates summer blockbuster pitches how to bring equality to the industry, and it belched, "Hot chix jumping sideways with two guns. PS—Please kill me."

It's mindless murder-porn, or, as my excellent friend John Skipp astutely coined it, *stupography*: media consciously devised to leave you outraged, excited, empowered, and dumber than you were before you watched it. And thank gods for that, because if Hollywood thinks a callow Silly Putty swipe at peak-Scorsese gravitas like *Joker* is a deep think-piece on violence in society, then stick to murder-porn, please. As a winking indictment of white incel rage, *Joker* almost satisfies; but if you saw yourself in this ham-fisted apotheosis of blighted entitlement fantasies, then brother, I'm sincerely worried about you, and I sure hope you get laid soon.

And speaking of sex...

Goddamnit, we need more serious erotic cinema that frankly explores sexuality itself. *The Cook, The Thief, His Wife And Her Lover. Tie Me Up, Tie Me Down.* Shit, even *The Secretary or Showgirls*. One reason sex continues to be more problematic than violence is the dicey nature of faking it. While few actors have come forward to speak of being traumatized by feigning violent death (injury or death does occur with appalling frequency to stuntpeople, who seldom rate more than a brief entertainment news item and never derail production) the experience of participating in a sex scene in front of a full crew and a tyrannical director can be almost as traumatic as off-screen sexual assault.

Game Of Thrones broke a dam in frankly depicting sex in an adult fantasy program, but seemed to have chronic problems with letting female characters enjoy it. Only recently have new policies, such as the welcome addition of intimacy coordinators—think stunt coordinator, only horizontal—begun to insure that actors can be comfortable with nudity and simulated sex on-camera. But even so, sex in film and TV these days must be dark and meaningful, which means prostitutes, strippers, adultery and rape... and violence.

It's getting so you almost want to turn off the TV and read a book. But wait...

Violence and sex on the printed page is only less stigmatized than other media because of the nigh-impenetrable firewall of you-have-to-read-it, but reading prose makes it a far more intimate and affecting forum for exploring unfulfilled desires, as well as a place to unpack our unaddressed fascination for these extremes of sensation.

Science fiction and fantasy have frequently led the way, but for every pioneer who brought mature insight to gender and sexual issues (see Theodore Sturgeon's *Godbody*, Ursula K. LeGuin's *The Left Hand Of Darkness* or Harlan Ellison's *Love Ain't Nothing But Sex Misspelled*), you had creeps like Heinlein, John Norman or Piers Anthony, preaching liberation of women as more accessible objects. If there was progress, it all too often was in the wrong ways, such as Marion Zimmer Bradley proving you don't have to have a dick to be a predator.

And what about violence? Military sf and sword and sorcery are still churning out the raypunk action porn; even the most cerebral hard sf still has to have an intergalactic war to prove its weighty bona fides, every fantasy series a modicum of swashbuckling and massive battle scenes. In horror, the quiet vs. extreme feud prevails over a bifurcated genre that seldom looks beyond its own appetite for more or fewer squishy adjectives to interrogate the troubling obligatory nature of rapine and pillage itself. Seldom outside of bizarro or the gentrified suburbs of the New Weird is the reader's need for vicarious carnage turned around for serious examination, but I fervently commend Norman Spinrad's *The Iron Dream* as a splendid satire of golden age pulp that skewers the toxic catharsis of fantasy violence as a scratch for genocidal itches.

We believe that sex is a wholesome, vital ingredient in life and art, and should bear far less burden in justifying itself than its strange bedfellow, violence. Longtime readers of *Forbidden Futures* already know all too well how shy we're not with sex and violence, but for this special issue, we gave our esteemed contributors free rein to explore the issue with no holds barred, but with an eye towards greater agency, wider representation and more conscious pornography. The result may not be to everyone's tastes, but we reserve the right to offend, and as always, we welcome your outrage.

And as with every story in every issue, we had to ask ourselves, "How far is too far?" With no standard to abide by beyond our own easily excitable appetites, we relied upon the wisdom of former Attorney General and noted pornography connoisseur Ed Meese, who famously said, "I know it when I see it." And as FF contributor and legendary literary vulgarian Ed Lee puts it, *"Mankind evolved to rule the earth because he is very violent and very sexual. These are ancient components of human dynamics, and those components linger ever as we have developed into sophisticated, civilized beings."**

A-fucking-men.

*— (*Interview with 52 Weeks Of Horror/ https://www.52weeksofhorror.com/single-post/2018/03/05/Screaming-Through-the-Flesh---An-Interview-with-Edward-Lee)*

UNKLE KRUST'S GUIDE TO FEMALE LADY-TYPES

—Not really manic, but will totally eat your dreams.
—Not really poly, just wants to nail your girl friend.
—Dust is actually no more magical than ordinary girl dust.
—Licked the deodorant you (should've) used this morning.

—Invites you to contribute blood to her fundraiser.
—Agelessly beautiful, but her hidden MySpace profile looks like your grandmother with leprosy.
—Reduced to feeding on victims remotely via coronavirus hoax memes.
—If you can't handle her draining your vital essence until you're a shriveled husk, you don't deserve her genital herpes.

—Posts devastating stories of hardship she's bravely endured overhearing her servants tell each other.
—Still sharing bondage cosplay selfies from that one time she almost felt sexy.
—Looking for serious life-partner to shovel her unicorn's shit.
—Secret kinks: auto-erotic asphyxiation, morbidly obese space slugs.

Q♦ — SWORD VIXEN

—Nifty leather outfit made from the skins of annoying bards.
—Traumatized by and sworn to avenge this thing she saw on YouTube ten minutes ago.
—Sends dick pics, but it's really just a necklace of severed dicks.
—Secret weakness: guys who collect vintage toys but never take them out of the box.

J♣ — ENCHANTRESS

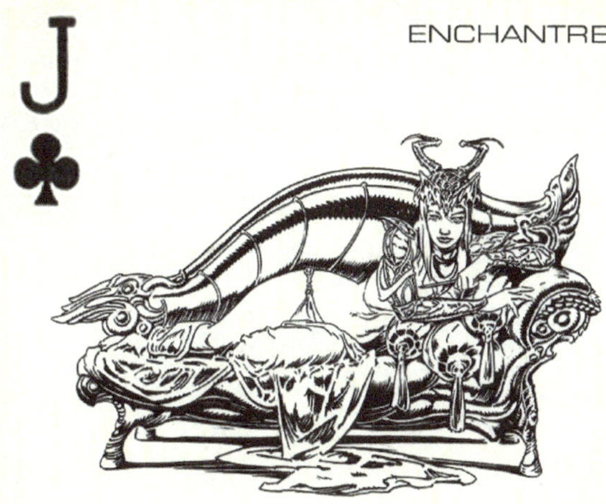

—Hoarding all the toilet paper to mummify you later.
—Turns your crew into pigs, cows and chickens; throws one hell of a BBQ.
—Hypnotizes you with endless anecdotes about how awesome all her exes were.
—Just looking for someone real enough to genuinely see through the enchantment to the soulless narcissist within, and blindly worship it forever.

7♠ — MERMAID

—Has crabs, will travel.
—Bombards you with inspirational karaoke rendition of "Wind Beneath My Wings," Venmo donation requests.
—Gets pregnant at social distancing parties.
—Not-so-secret foot fetish.

Q♠ — SPACE-PIRATESS

—Hijacks all the hand sanitizer.
—Always down for a serious argument about how astrology mischaracterizes Scorpios.
—Turn-ons: watching you fight to the death against your alternate-universe doppelganger.
—Don't even step to her if you can't do the Kessel Run in thirty parsecs or less.

FORBIDDEN FUTURES 7

THE DAMSEL OF DESIRE
GREGORY BOSSERT

THE DENIZENS OF THE CHATTEL pens of Qual lived in squalor, rage, and despair. All, that is, but two.

Throm and Malamalama lived in each other.

This was true figuratively. Their brief fierce joys and slow slender hopes, the depth of their slumber in the dank dark and the vigor of their waking to the thrallmaster's bell, and most of all their fury and grace and continual success in the staged battles that were the delight of the Seventy-Third Theomancer of Qual: all these came from within the improbable love that had grown between them in their years in the pens.

And this was true literally. For every moment that the broad barbarian from the mountainous West and the towering demoness from the Eastern desert were not asleep or in combat in the arena they spent entwined in a passion deeply and thoroughly carnal. There was no orifice that they had not been explored to conclusion, no extremity from nail to tail not inserted to its length, no effuse not liberally applied inside and out.

The Theomancer of Qual himself would brave the dank depths of pens in sorcerous disguise to view the lovers in flagrante or to hang batlike above them as they slumbered, still embedded in each other and swaddled within Malamalama's wide wings. His unnatural addiction to this voyeuristic study outweighed his natural cruelty which would have long before had him send the two lovers into the arena together, for only one of the combatants who entered that bloody place together was allowed out again alive.

Further incentive to the couple's preservation came from the Theomancer's surprising success with a series of illustrated chapbooks cataloging the pair's most carnal excesses. He had found a steady source of income and a wary social acceptance among the most discerning elite from the sale of these volumes, as well as the attention—not entirely welcomed by the reclusive wizard—of the notoriously decadent débutante, the Suzerainesse a'Yama-Voni.

The Suzerainesse had been peerless in perversity before our two lovers's rise to fame, and she was able to get past the Theomancer's awkward dismissals due to two facts: First, she had achieved some sort of libidinous release with beings of every natural genus and no few unnatural; the Theomancer's wizened form was no great deterrent to one who had mounted the termite mounds of the eastern desert or crawled the length of the Worm of Cram from rear to front. And second, the Suzerainesse was motivated not by lust but by something far simpler, which was a deadly jealousy.

OVER THE SPACE OF A YEAR the Suzerainesse ingratiated of herself into the Theomancer's studies and amusements until she had run of his palace and, eventually, access to the schedule of his arena.

It was in that arena one humid midsummer evening that the Suzerainesse ran razor nails up the Theomancer thigh, leaving dotted staves of blood on his pale paperish skin, and said, "My dear, you will forgive me if, inspired by my great admiration of your investigations into the limits of the erotic, I have arranged my own modest attempt at an entertainment."

"Ah, well, of course, my esteemed, uh, colleague and, erm, fellow aficionado," the wizard stuttered. "I look forward to your, ah, ingenuity."

Two robed and hooded figures were lead into the arena, and weapons placed into their hands. It was clear from the way that the fighters stumbled with arms outstretched that they were blinded by the hoods and likely drugged to boot. The two spent some while staggering about, swords slashing at air, while the Theomancer muttered a few unconvincing commendations to the Suzerainesse; he had frankly been expecting something with many more bodies and much more skin.

The two combatants finally found each other and began to battle. Slash by slash they stripped away each others robes and tore into the exposed flesh underneath. The hoods, made of stout leather that covered eyes, ears, and mouth, were the last to give way, and so it was that the audience became aware of the identity of the fighters before they did themselves.

They were, of course, Throm and Malamalama.

The Theomancer was both dismayed and delighted by this revelation. His disappointment at losing this long-time source of entertainment and income was balanced by the hope that with the couple finally split asunder, as it were, he would be free to return to his studies unbothered by distractions...such as the Suzerainesse a'Yama-Voni.

He kept these thoughts to himself, however, out of respect for his colleague, all the more so as her nails, which were literally razors pinned to her fingertips, were now firmly ensconced around his testicles.

After a brutal hour of blind battle the flow of blood inside and out had flushed the drugs from the combatants' minds and the two were able to free themselves from the hoods.

"My love," the two cried in unison. They crashed together in blood-slicked embraced, then held each other at arms length to survey each others wounds, which were grisly but not yet fatal.

"I should have been able to catch some scent of you, or sense the rhythm of your heart which as familiar to me as my own, hood or not," the demoness moaned.

"And I should have recognized you by the touch of your beloved claws upon my skin," the barbarian answered.

They embraced once more, with a kiss as ferocious as their previous combat, and then spun apart, weapons high.

Throm addressed the guards that lined the outer edge of the arena, but those guards were heavily armored and held tridents that were thrice the length of the barbarian's swing. Weakened by a dozen wounds, the barbarian finally fell to his knees.

Malamalama in the meanwhile attempted to ascend to the balcony from which the Theomancer and Suzerainesse watched. Even though her wings had been broken so thoroughly when she'd been captured that she could never fly again, she flailed them now with such determination that the demoness almost cleared the railing before cartilage and tendon gave way and she plummeted back to the sand below.

"Tell me again, my dear," the Suzerainesse said in a voice that cut the sudden silence. "What is the rule that you so wisely and wonderfully set for these magnificent battles?"

The Theomancer winced as her fingers shifted. "Only one may, ah, exit alive."

Throm and Malamalama clutched each other in the gore-soaked sand.

"We will die together," the barbarian said, "for surely our love is so great that we will meet again in the afterlife for all of eternity."

But the demoness shook her great horned head. "The afterlife of my people is an endless cyclone of fire through which we soar in agonized bliss. My wings will be restored there, but your spirit would plummet to the flames below."

Throm groaned, "And that of my people is a never-ending hunt and, alas, you would without doubt be the hunted."

"And so you must kill me and live," Malamalama said, "and spare us that fate."

"Exactly," Throm said, "but it is you that must kill me."

"No!" the demoness cried, and lunged forward toward the barbarian's blade.

"Yes!" cried the barbarian, slipping sideways to take Malamalama's claws into his shoulder.

And so now started the battle anew, but inverted, as the two lovers used all their skills to attempt to impale themselves upon the other. Throm tried to drop his blade, but the demoness snatched it and almost managed to skewer herself by pressing the hilt against his chest, so he was forced to snatch it back from her.

Malamalama bore no weapon beyond her own claws and teeth and terrible strength, and so it was to her the victory, terrible as it was, finally fell, for she could retract her claws and close her wide mouth, but the barbarian had no place to sheath his sword except within the demoness's flesh. Throm's hand slipped for no more than an instant but Malamalama seized the moment—and the sword—and threw herself upon it.

Wrapping her arms and wings around Throm, she forced herself down the blade to give him one last kiss. "Live, my love, until you find some way that we can be united in death." Then she raised her head and howled and fell backward in the sand.

Throm bent over her body a moment, gently washing the gore from her face with his tears.

Then with a howl that equaled Malamalama's, Throm ripped his sword from her chest. He plunged his hand into the gaping hole and pulled out her heart, held it high as he staggered toward the balcony, his hate and anguish so powerful that the Theomancer fell back in his throne and even the Suzerainesse flinched.

"Keep this as a remembrance," Throm snarled. "Both of the beauty of her flesh and the certainty that I shall return and send you each to your own hideous hells."

He hurled the heart into the Theomancer's lap. The wizard clutched the organ, which fully the size of his head, and felt what he thought at the time was inspiration.

"A remembrance it shall be," the Theomancer cried. "Of the transience of passion, for the only undying thing is knowledge itself. Bring me the casket from my desk!"

This receptacle held the heart of his older brother, who had been Seventy-Second Theomancer of Qual before his untimely demise from a poisoned papercut. The current Theomancer had fortuitously been closeted nearby and was able to salvage the heart. He kept it displayed in a small glass chest on his desk to, as he said, "preserve my brother's memory." In fact, not just the memories but the old Theomancer's vital spirit itself had been trapped in that shriveled meat, soundlessly screaming in tormented rage. The greeting the current Theomancer gave the heart in its casket each morning was a pleasure second only to his now truncated study of our two lovers.

The casket having been fetched, the Theomancer unsealed it and grasped the wretched organ inside. To it he whispered, "Farewell, brother. I release you from this little hell to the greater one below," and then tossed it aside; the Suzerainesse plucked it from the air and bit into it with her rows of rusted-needle teeth as if it were a ripened pear.

The Theomancer placed Malamalama's heart into the casket, thrilling as the demoness's entrapped spirit began to wake into agony. It occurred to him that imprisoning Throm's soul alongside his lover's would perfect that delight, but when he looked up to order the barbarian's slaughter, the Theomancer discovered the arena's guards slain and the doors in splintered ruin.

He turned to the Suzerainesse, who was wiping thick blackened gore from her chin. She shrugged and cupped the Theomancer's cheek with slick fingers. "Let the cretin run," she said. "His guilt shall be torment enough. Come, let us turn to finer pursuits."

THROM CUT HIS way out of the arena to the main gate. The guards at the latter took one look at his blood-drench, rage-ravaged face and retreated to the safety of the barbican, returning after several minutes had passed to lock the gates against his possible return. The folks of the surrounding town slammed their doors and shutters against his grievous howling.

And so Throm ran.

For seven days straight he ran, never deviating from the line that had lead from the Theomancer's arena. Seven days straight across roads and fields, not stopping for food or sleep, taking only what water fell into his mouth as he screamed into the passing storms.

Seven days straight out of the lands of Qual and into the northern hills, a region of dim forests hung grey with moss where even the living trees crumbled with rot and the soil shifted and slithered underfoot.

Those few who ventured that forest did so in search of mushrooms, which thrived in that dank gloom, and which could be sold for generous sums to doctors, drug-fiends, and patrons of the dark arts; the Theomancer was a reliable consumer on all three fronts. These fruiting bodies were the visible expression of an underground web of mycelia that stretched for unmeasured miles in all directions, an interwoven net of such complexity as to have developed a strange sort of self-awareness.

It was into a ring of such fungi that Throm finally collapsed, of a type known to only the most adventuresome of collectors, who had dubbed them the Damsel of Desire.

The species had evolved in symbiosis with certain wasps; to the wasps it gave unusual vigor and a clarity of focus, and from the wasps it took the form of a special motile fruiting body. These free-flying organs took on the wasp's form and function, allowing it to infiltrate the wasp nest before disintegrating into spores and thus ensuring its distribution to new regions of the forest.

On rare occasion this species would infect a bird or mammal instead, taking on its shape and purpose. Indeed, the forest foxes had learned to nap in its circles, acquiring both its rejuvenating effects and a temporary fungal ally, a sort of foxfruit that could accompany them for days before bursting.

And more rarely yet the fungus had melded with a person, granting them youth and a sort doppelgänger, not of exact form but rather of shared purpose. There were few, however, with the skill to find the Damsel of Desire and the courage to lie down within its ring. But through some uncanny fate, this was what Throm had now done.

And it was as fate, or rather Fates, that the fungus came to Throm. His thoughts spun like a whirlwind. Or no, he was still and the whirlwind spun around him, slowly resolving itself into three forms of extraordinary beauty: sheer sweeping wings, fangs that shimmered like opal, claws that arced like the cres-

cent moon, eyes as black and boundless as the darkest midnight. Between the three figures stretched the glimmering silver strands that were the fungus's true self.

Throm was not surprised that the Fates had taken the image of his beloved, nor that they had chosen that of her perfect youth in the desert before she had ever learned of the world of men. What better form in which to give him final oblivion he desired.

He thought that desire was about to be fulfilled, as the three Fates spiraled in around him, wings and claws and fangs drawing ever closer. Imagine then his surprise when that swirling embrace did not tear, but rather, caressed. Imagine his bewilderment when those glistening teeth parted not to shriek outrage at his guilt, but rather to whisper gentle enticements, and to reveal serpentine tongues that probed his torn flesh. Imagine his abashment when his body aroused itself to this thrice-mirrored image of his dead lover, the six-fold stroke of hand and foot and breast and thigh, the fainter tracing of the fungal web that linked the three.

The three Fates spoke, passing the words each to each as they orbited around him in that dreamspace.

"—the body perhaps too close to death even for our powers to restore—"

"—but the spirit strong enough to bring that broken body here to us—"

"—so think then how far and wide his desire could spread our spore—"

"—were we to mend this tattered cloak of flesh—"

"—and take its pattern for our own—"

"—but look, this flesh already shrouds two spirits, one born to it—"

"—and one welcomed in so deeply that his thoughts are half hers—"

"—and his lips, his bowels, his blood itself holds her mortal traces—"

"—the point where one blends to the other as undefined as are our own connections—"

"—and where two abide so strongly there is surely room for three—"

"—and so he shall live and she in him and we in them."

At that the Fates caresses became more urgent, the probings of their claws and wingtips and tongues more intimate, their orbit ever tighter.

And in the world outside, Throm's body slowly sank into the soil as mycelial tendrils invaded every opening, and spiraled up to wrap his ever more engorged manhood. His body was soon entirely cocooned by this fungal growth, just as his dreaming spirit was wrapped in the Fates' wanton gyrations. When body and spirit alike finally swirled up to climax that cocoon shook like jelly and then settled, as if the entirety of Throm's encapsulated flesh had been consumed and released in that fountaining.

Ten days passed, then, as Throm's spirit floated in blissful blankness and the fungus reconstructed him from his desire. A fox stopped to sniff around the mound at the center of the ring and then fled to tell its fellows that the Damsel of Desire was at work on its magnum opus.

At dawn on the eleventh day a tendril sprouted from the mound, and from that tendril a fruiting body grew. It was at first a simple orb, wrinkled like a brain partitioned not into two parts but three. By evening it had gown into its final form, which was that the Fates had taken within Throm's mind, a youthful dream of the demoness Malamalama, lithe and long-winged. And at midnight, suffused with the distilled desire of barbarian and demoness and fungus, the fruiting body of the Damsel of Desire stretched its wings, squatted to snap the tendril that held it to its parents, then leapt into the sky. It loop once, twice, then soared southward toward the palace of the Theomancer of Qual.

THE FOLLOWING DAY, the mound in the center of the ring of mushrooms split and withered. Throm sat up, dug dirt and the residue of dream from his eyes, staggered to his feet. His balance was off, his sense of self baffled and skewed. It took the better part of an hour for him accept the evidence of his senses; not only was he alive, and rejuvenated to the smooth sinewed strength of his youth, but he had somehow acquired a pair of wings.

Throm sat for a while and thought, while the foxes came one by one to gaze unseen at the Damsel's masterwork.

"I could head to the Eastern desert and confess Malamalama's kin of her fate at my hand," he thought. "But she had no kind words for her people while she was alive, and I fear that they will not mourn but rather celebrate her death. Or I could return to my clan in the mountainous West, but they are an uncouth lot, as likely to mock my sorrow as they are to commiserate. Or I could head north to find what oblivion lies beyond this forest, but that would be to deny this second chance the Fates have given me, and never they grant a third."

And so, not trusting himself to flight, he tucked his wings behind him, rescued his sword from the undergrowth, and began to walk south.

SO UNRECOGNIZABLE WAS Throm, between his renewed youth and his wings, that the very guards who had fled from him just the month before now taunted him for his temerity in approaching the Theomancer's gate. After a thorough beating they tossed him into the chattel pens.

It was a custom of the thrallmaster to pit the latest acquisitions against each other to get a better idea of their capabilities. And so it was just a day later that Throm found himself entering the arena once more, as thoroughly disguised by his transformation has he had been the last time by robe and hood. His plan was to dispatch his opponent quickly but simply, with no flourish that might reveal his identity or excite the thrallmaster's attention. The success of his revenge relied on his lying low.

Or so he thought. That changed when his opponent entered the ring, and all his thoughts fled. For here was the Damsel of Desire's strange fruiting body, the very image his dear Malamalama's youthful self.

"My love?" he asked.

The lovely vision extended one perfect pearlescent claw.

"Throm," she said.

The audience gasped. The Theomancer, who had been reading a book through the usually dull initial matches, squinted down at the two.

"What game is this now?" he asked the Suzerainesse, who shrugged.

Throm looked up at the two on the balcony. "Yes, it is I, Throm of the mountainous West, reborn and returned to take my vengeance!" His plan, such as it was, having been thwarted by the unaccountable appearance of his deceased lover, he threw his hopes wholly onto the gift of the Fates and the untested strength of his wings.

"Rise with me, my love," he said, and with great uneven flaps lifted himself into the air.

The Theomancer shrieked. The Suzerainesse gestured frantically to the guards, though they were far fewer and less well armed than those she had arranged for Throm's previous appearance.

Throm's opponent shook back her long tangled mane and unfurled her own wings, a single stroke of which sufficed to raise her next to Throm.

"Why were their wings not broken?" the Suzerainesse snarled at the thrallmaster. In fact, the thrallmaster had determined that Throm's wings were insufficient to support his weight, and she had personally smashed the joints of the young demoness. This seemed too much to impart to the Suzerainesse in the moment, however, so the thrallmaster instead turned and ran.

The Suzerainesse would have run as well if the Theomancer had not wrapped his spindly arms about her waist. She shoved at his arms as if slipping out of a skirt, but as he had also managed to get his legs around her ankles she gave up and wrenched herself around to face her certain doom.

The reborn barbarian and the mysterious demoness had met in the air above the arena, just opposite the balcony. Throm, hovering unsteadily, braced himself on the shoulders of the other and gazed lovingly into her eyes.

And then he cried out and pushed himself back.

"That face is surely that of my beloved Malamalama," he said. "But those eyes..."

"Yes," the other said. "these eyes are your own. Are they not, Father?" She reached out with one lovely hand to grip Throm's shoulder. The other she plunged wrist-deep into Throm's chest.

The two plummeted to the arena floor. The Suzerainesse dragged herself and the Theomancer to the railing to look down at them, just in time to see the young demoness rise up with Throm's heart clasped between curved claws.

"And so do I fulfill your desire," the creature said to the barbarian's body, not unkindly, and then rose up into the air again.

"Guards," the Suzerainesse grunted, but they had fled. She tried to drag herself back from the railing but the Theomancer had snared himself on one of the spikes. She hissed through her needle teeth and looked up to discover the creature hovering before her, the barbarian's heart held out in one perfect hand.

"You have earned this," the creature said. Trembling, the Suzerainesse took the heart in her own twisted, steel-edged fingers. The faux demoness drifted forward, her head tilting back, her lovely crimson lips stretching around her fangs in an expression of such absolute orgasmic fulfillment that the Suzerainesse was certain that the creature was about to rip her limb from limb.

But it was the demoness who burst asunder, not with a scream and a shower of gore, but with a gentle pop and the scent of loam under leaves, into a million floating spores.

THE SUZERAINESSE WAS half-minded to lift the Theomancer over the railing and drop him down into the arena. But he redeemed himself by snatching Throm's heart from her and rushing it to his study, where with a few muttered words he sealed the heart into the glass casket on his desk beside Malamalama's own.

"And so shall these two lovers dwell in agony, so close and yet unable to touch, until their spirits dissolve into madness as thoroughly, just as their unnatural child dissipated into no more compost."

So sneering was this statement, so delightedly cruel the sentiment behind it, that the Suzerainesse's annoyance metamorphosed into lust. In a single motion she stripped the wizard's robe from his body and sent him flying to the floor. With one flick of razor nails she sliced away her own dress, and with another she grazed his already half-erect member to full trembling height. Then she dropped, impaling herself upon him with such force that the breath was knocked out of him, literally and figuratively.

And so the two were oblivious to the transformation happening just over their heads. For inside the glass casket, pale tendrils grew from the barbarian's spore-spangled heart to embrace that of the demoness, and after a moment, more of the same sprouted gleaming from Malamalama's heart to entwince themselves back around Throm's. The two hearts pulled themselves closer, tendrils gently interweaving, until the flesh itself began to meld.

The two on the floor had rolled halfway under the desk by then, the Suzerainesse having pinned the Theomancer to the floor with one nail through an earlobe, and so they remained unaware even as the hearts sent a stout stalk upward, shattering the glass, growing ever longer and thicker until it flowered into a fruiting body of such extraordinary sensual beauty, such sheer erotic power that the Theomancer and Suzerainesse could not help but notice it as it descended. Indeed, the two might have worked up another bestselling chapbook from a description of this loveliest creation of the Damsel of Desire, had they survived its coming.

AS FOR WHAT BECAME of Throm and Malamalama after this fruiting, no serious scholarly work can say. But the barbarians of the mountainous West tell a tale of their afterlife, that endless hunt, of how two beauteous beings can sometime be glimpsed by the most courageous and passionate of the dead, but never captured. And the demons of the Eastern desert will speak—to those few strangers that they spare—of how, far above the cyclone of fire that is their own final fate, two figures soar so entwined they seem as one.

SEX AND VIOLENCE

FORBIDDEN FUTURES 7
INCUBUS
SUCCUBUS
IAMBUS
MICHAEL ALLEN ROSE
18

THE DAY THE HUMANS DIED WAS QUITE A COUP
WITH NO ONE LEFT TO FUCK THEY HAD TO TRY
TO FIND A WAY TO FILL THEIR DIRTY HOLES
AND TURN THE WRATH OF SIN AGAINST THE SKY

The human race was dead. Their cities lay in ruin. Their great works, things that marked their presence, swept away and forgotten.

After the human apocalypse, the Earth bounced back quickly, reinvigorated by the shedding of God's favorite creation. In the absence of mankind, canopies of trees shot up into the sky, animals thrived unmolested, and even the air itself had begun the long process of recovery.

Hell, on the other hand, had become more hellish than ever. Belial could attest to this. The literal hell—the sinister realm of which his grandfather, for whom he was named, was a prince of rot and ruin—had become a Hell of ennui, malaise, and boredom.

This Belial was an incubus, or had been before the fall of mankind, spending his days enjoying the fruits of hell's amenities reserved only for the elite, and his nights elbow-deep in mortal orifices.

He sat on a cliff overlooking a river of magma, next to his friend Vual, a succubus. Undone by the lack of human mortals available for torture, she pined for the times she'd sharpened her art of seduction to a razor's edge and slid it beneath the thumbnails and across the meatus of any fool who dared welcome her lusty embrace.

She fondly remembered the many hot nights when she would slither unbidden into someone's bed and their dreams until they were fit to rupture like a cum-stuffed tick. Upon waking from such depths of circadian arousal, they would debase themselves and beg to sign her contract. It was the corruption that turned her on - knowing that for a moment of pleasure, mortals would happily damn themselves to an eternity festering in the putrid pits below.

Now, there was nothing to do but reminisce. The damned and the saved were off limits, entombed in chambers of eternal punishment or free to roam the golden fields of Heaven. Few humans were considered worthy of salvation; Belial and Vual had been part of an army that made sure of it. Either way, all mortals had passed, all souls sorted.

Most demonic entities had found other work after the fall of man, many taking up the positions of torturers. Demons that caused mortals to murder, for example, turned to making them feel pain in the afterlife, their violence inflicted on their own bodies

again and again. Demons of excess and indulgence filled the stomachs, livers and assholes of damned pleasure-seekers to bursting and beyond. Belial and Vual were not like the demons of lust, who were reveling in eternal an orgy of genital mutilation. They had more specialized occupations, and were now obsolete.

Vual ran her nails down Belial's muscular flank, drawing dark, inky blood. Her forked tongue flicked lasciviously as he growled. "I think I'm going insane. Let's just try it together. See how it tastes."

Belial considered his options. They had often spoken of trying to get some satisfaction from each other. There were few more experienced at the art of sexual pleasure than incubi and succubi, so it followed their congress would be epic and unspeakable. This, however, was something never done before. Neither knew what would happen if they fucked.

"Let us… try."

The prurient carnage that followed was visceral, base, and deliciously evil. Belial and Vual plied their skills expertly, using their encyclopedic knowledge of all philias, fetishes, and possible proclivities to craft a sort of mental map. They followed this document like explorers in a new world, pursuing every tributary to the very end of sensation and sanity.

Demonic analogues of every bodily fluid were spilled. Orifices gaped. Protrusions smashed against one another. Wings, horns, and pointed tails did unspeakable things in the service of hedonism. After what seemed like an eternity, Vual stopped, mid-thrust, her vaginal fangs retracting and growing soft.

Belial removed his unholy poker from her snatch, bringing forth a torrent of blood and discharge. "Is that yours or mine?"

"Does it matter?" asked Vual as she bent forward, practically in half, to run her tongue along his shaft and lap up the viscous fluid suspended between them. She squeezed his bulbous testicles with a deft hand, bringing purple, throbbing veins to the surface, pumping fiery jism like an engine of war. She sighed, idly punishing his sac. "This is… not gratifying."

He exhaled like a chorus of deflating balloons. "Something is missing. I'm enjoying myself, but…"

Neither wanted to say it aloud, but Vual choked it out first, the thought occurring as a brightly flashing sun at the center of her being: "Corruption. That's the thing."

"Corruption," purred Belial. "A once abundant resource, and now…"

They both knew it to be true. That deliciousness was lost in their coupling. The heady sensation of damning a human soul to an eternity of pain and horror surpassed any orgasm. The moment the deal was struck, Belial and Vual could actually hear the breaking of the human spirit. Like a stick of candy, it provided a sweet rush of endorphins to their demonic bodies.

"It's a lost cause. There aren't any mortals left.

"There's no way to access them in the beyond. We would have to get past countless angels."

Belial snorted, setting a passing insect aflame. "Get past them? What, are they to attack us with their flaming swords? Hurl us into the abyss? They've done all that. They have grown soft and weak, spending eternity threatening mortals with things we have already experienced."

"We didn't make the rules, and yet we're bound by them? Fucking angels… they know not what they're missing. If only we could show them." Vual stared at her fellow demon, letting the words hang in the air, pregnant with meaning.

Belial was silent. His eyes shone with an inner glow, like the heart of a flame. Slowly, he revealed his fangs in a tentative grin. "Are you suggesting a raid on Heaven?"

"Perhaps."

"It's impossible. Never been done."

Vual thought for a moment. "So what? Neither had the Apocalypse, until it was so…"

When Jophiel answered Heaven's door, he looked stunned.

"The seraphim known for being most beautiful, what a surprise," purred Vual, winding her pointed tail around his brightly glowing, muscular thigh.

"Can I help you?" asked the angel, his voice thick with authority.

"May we borrow a cup of sugar?" asked Belial, his eyes sparkling. A seraphim would be a tough nut to crack, being so high up in heaven's hierarchy, but Satan himself had once been a seraph.

Jophiel didn't quite know what to do. This was highly irregular, and he said so, but it didn't matter to the pair of demons now intoxicating him with infernal pheromones.

"In the name of God, I demand that you submit to his holy—"

"You know so little of submission," said Vual. "We will teach you."

Resistance began and ended with a stamped foot and a hard "no," but there was no soul at stake, only the shame and delicious guilt that would pump from the angel's throbbing soul when the deed had been completed. The angels had grown apathetic and listless, their powers waning and their guard lowered. It took only a few licentious whispers and a clawed finger under the seraph's skirts before all Jophiel's defenses broke.

The blasphemies that came from Jophiel's mouth that day rocked Heaven. They left him, many hours later, covered in fluids, rocking back and forth, and muttering how the filth coating his wings would never come off.

Like noxious oil soaking into a scrap of linen, the plague of lust began to spread almost immediately. A third of the host had been cast out of Heaven at the beginning of time, and some who were spared by the first judgment found themselves curious about the pleasures of the flesh denied them for so many epochs. Various angels tried to overcome the spreading sexual hysteria of the incubi with exorcism, sacramental confession, the sign of the cross, attempted excommunications, and simply hiding. Unfortunately, Franciscan friar Ludovico Maria Sinistrari had been correct when he stated that incubi *"have no dread of exorcisms and show no reverence for holy things."* If anything, the angels' desperate attempts to stem the plague of lust only made everyone hornier, as the sin tally increased exponentially. The taboo was a particularly effective aphrodisiac.

"We have discovered a new purpose, sister," Belial chuckled, removing an angel's holy genitalia from his mouth just long enough to laugh.

Vual was currently beating the backs of two cherubim with the twisted body of a throne. Starlight leaked out from their greedy wounds and vaporized into mist as the creatures began to orgasm, sending cosmic matter flying. "Indeed. Let us make an appointment with God, soon. I believe he needs to relax, don't you?"

The universe would choke and gasp with one last spurt of blood and cum, before expiring.

MAN THOUGHT THAT HIS DAMNATION, HE'D AVOID
BUT SUCCUBI AND INCUBI, ATTEND
YOUR ENERGY COMBINED, THE ANGELS WEEP
THE UNIVERSE GETS FUCKED UNTIL THE END

SEX AND VIOLENCE

GREEN SUITS

BY JEFF STRAND

Cliff shifted in his seat in the back of the van. "This suit is too tight in the crotch. I get that my girth is abnormally large, but still, I'm feeling really constricted here."

"Quiet," said Bradley. "We need to focus. Get in the zone."

"I can't get in the zone when my dick is suffocating. Was this designed for somebody with a micro-phallus? Did anybody bring scissors so I can cut out a hole and get some circulation going?"

"I told you to focus."

"Focus on what?" asked Cliff. "Since when do bank robbers need to get in the zone? I've done this a bunch of times. We wave our guns, tell them to hand over the cash, and we get out. I don't want to be Zen. How can I threaten to kill people if I'm feeling at peace with the earth and the constellations and shit?"

"I didn't say we need to be in a Zen state. I said we need to focus. What if an off-duty cop is in line and because you're not focused you don't realize that he's taken out his gun? Will you be more focused when he pulls the trigger and splatters your brains all over the poor bank teller?"

"Brain."

"What?"

"Brain. Singular. I only have one brain."

"I said it right," said Bradley. "I know you only have one brain, but 'splatters your brains' is correct."

"It may be common usage, but it's not correct," said Cliff. "Sorry, it's just a pet peeve of mine. You can't bash somebody's skull against the pavement until their brains leak out when they only have one brain. If you were torturing somebody to get information, you wouldn't cut his noses off. One nose. One brain."

Bradley frowned. "I think maybe it becomes plural when it's in pieces."

"We could Google it."

"No! We're supposed to be focusing! And you're not supposed to have your phone with you!"

"I don't. It's not like there'd be any room for it in this ugly tight-ass suit anyway."

They rode in silence for a moment.

"What are you moping about?" Cliff asked Franklin, who was seated across from him, staring at the floor of the van.

"Nothing."

"You look like you're pouting about something."

"Nah."

"What's wrong?" Cliff persisted. "You seemed so upbeat when we were getting our instructions for this job. I figured you were looking forward to shoving your gun into some innocent faces. You strike me as somebody who gets off on scaring people. No judgment—just saying that I assumed you were a psychopath."

"It's not ugly," said Franklin.

"What? The suit?"

"I designed them myself. We look good in them. Like a team."

"Shit. I didn't know you designed them."

"When people worry about whether their money is safe at their financial institution, I want them unable to shake the mental image of our matching green suits. FDIC insured or not, they know we're coming for their hard-earned cash. We're not just robbing one bank, we're eroding consumer confidence in the entire banking system!"

"I admire your ambition," said Cliff. "But the suit is still too tight in the crotch."

"Well, I had to guess at the size."

"You guessed wrong. It's a lovely shade of green, though. Well done."

"I can't tell if you're being sarcastic," said Franklin.

"I was being sarcastic, but while I was saying it I decided that I legitimately did like the color, so I went from sarcastic to sincere in one breath. Why'd you go with green?"

Franklin shrugged. "It just seemed like the most sinister color."

"Are you out of your damn mind?" asked Bradley.

Cliff and Franklin looked over at him.

"I'm sorry," said Bradley, "our focus is obviously destroyed at this point, so I might as well say what's on my mind. Green is the stupidest color you could have chosen for these suits."

"Don't you like green?"

"I love green. Green is a delightful color. You know who's green? Kermit the Frog. He sang a whole frickin' classic song about his color."

"'It's Not Easy Being Green,'" said Cliff, helpfully.

"Right. He's a charming, beloved character. If you want a sinister color, you go with blood-red or pitch-black. Green isn't intimidating at all. It's soothing."

"What about Oscar the Grouch?" asked Franklin.

"I knew as soon as I brought up Kermit that you were going to do the whole 'What about Oscar the Grouch?' thing. Oscar is not a menacing character. Yeah, he's an asshole, but you don't *fear* him. You don't fear the Jolly Green Giant. You don't fear Yoda. You don't fear The Grinch. If you're trying to brand us as scary characters, green is the wrong color. Frickin' Greedo has this whole controversy because he got blown away so easily that they had to re-edit *Star Wars.* Gumby's not scary. Mike Wazowski, that short green one-eyed fucker from *Monsters Inc.*? Not scary at all, and he's a professional monster! Slimer isn't scary—he's funny! Shrek? The

Teenage Mutant Ninja Turtles? None of them are fearsome. People like green characters!"

"What about the Wicked Witch of the West?" asked Franklin.

"Fine," said Bradley. "Yes, the Wicked Witch of the West is responsible for millions of children crapping their pants in terror. It's the exception that proves the rule."

"What does that even mean?" asked Cliff. "I've never understood that phrase. How can an exception prove a rule?"

"If there's an exception, there must be a rule. Can't have exceptions without a rule. That's what the phrase means."

"I still don't get it. It's a dumb-ass phrase."

"Well, I'll be sure to give your feedback to the people who create phrases for the English language. Any other phrases that are beyond your understanding?"

"We're getting distracted," said Cliff.

"You're the one who started the distractions! I was trying to get us to focus! I was perfectly willing to let Franklin believe that his shitty green suits weren't a complete misfire! Even if the color was appropriate, what the hell kind of bank robbers coordinate their outfits? When the Big Man told us we had to wear these suits, I thought he was out of his damn mind! Never mind that they're ugly and don't fit right—it's a dumb idea!"

"Yours doesn't fit either?" asked Franklin, sounding forlorn.

"No. And unlike Mr. King Kong Dick here, my penis is just slightly above average in length and girth and this suit is *still* restricting my ability to have kids. It's a design flaw. These suits suck. Fuck you for designing them. How did you make this happen? Are you related to the Big Man or something?"

Franklin didn't respond.

"Holy crap, are you?"

"I'm his nephew."

"So your uncle assigned you to this job, and you said, 'Hey, wouldn't it be sweet if we were all in green suits that I personally designed?' and he said, 'Well, Nephew Franklin, that's the stupidest fucking idea I've heard all year, but hey, we're blood relatives, have it your way.' Is that what happened?"

"No."

"What part did I get wrong?" Bradley asked.

"None of it was right," said Franklin. "I mean, the basic gist was right, but you didn't get any of the dialogue right."

"I can't believe you think that wearing these dipshitty green suits is going to bring down the world's financial system. We're not even breaking into the safe. We're waving guns around like some low-rent hillbilly thugs and making them empty the cash drawers."

"Hey," said the van driver, turning around in his seat. "I didn't want to interrupt, but we've been at the bank for the past couple of minutes. You may want to go in there and rob it."

"I don't know if I can," said Cliff. "I'm feeling very unfocused."

Bradley reached into his pocket, took out a gun, and shot Cliff in the head, emptying much of his skull. Cliff slumped forward as chunks of gray matter slid down the inside of the van.

"Credit where it's due," Bradley told Franklin. "The pockets are very roomy."

Franklin said nothing.

"What do you think?" asked Bradley, pointing to the gore. "I blew his *brains* out, right? That's totally the correct usage."

"Yes," said Franklin in a very quiet voice. "I would've said brains, too."

"If his entire brain had jettisoned out of his skull in a single unit, yes, I would have blown his brain out. But look at it. There are, like, eight different blobs of it. Brains. Plural. One brain, two brains, three brains...well, I don't need to count all the way to eight. You get what I'm saying, right?"

"Uh-huh."

"As a rule, I don't murder my fellow bank robbers, so I guess Cliff is the exception that proves the rule! Ha!"

"So," said the van driver, "since we've discharged a firearm right in front of the bank, I feel like I should drive away now."

"Yeah, that's probably a good idea," said Bradley. "Not gonna lie—I was in no mental state to do this job in the first place. It's why I was trying so hard to focus. I needed this money to pay for my meds."

"Are you going to kill me too?" asked Franklin.

"Nope. Don't want your uncle getting pissed at me."

"Thanks."

"Wow, look at this way Cliff's blood is running right off the suit without staining it. Was that part of the design?"

"Yes. I thought some blood might spatter during the job."

"Nice work. I apologize for giving you crap about it before. I was just cranky."

"No problem. It's not easy being green."

FORBIDDEN
FUTURES

(K)NAIVETY

CRAIG LAURANCE GIDNEY

THE SPANGLETREES ON THE isle of Shaangö don't have leaves. The branches are stark and bare. But at dusk, in the crepuscular light, they issue a mist that shrouds everything in sparkling webs. The vaporous webs grow and glisten, full of metallic dust. The glittering dust settles and slowly vanishes, and by the next morning, it dissipates, burned off by the sun. No-one knows why or how the spangletrees produce this fog, part gossamer and part jewel-toned dust. No birds nest in the spangletrees, and animals avoid spangletree groves. Some locals avoid the spangletrees, due to superstition, and call them Witch Trees.

The only people who enter copses of spangletrees are thieves, magicians and perverts. Persons of low moral character congregate in the diaphanous wisps exhaled by the trees, to conduct their unsavory business.

Two such people were inside the swirling cloud on a particular evening, which was illuminated by moonlight. They prowled around the trunks. One of them carried a wand, shaped like a lighting bolt. The other had hair the color of night, contained in a braid wound with golden wire. Eventually, their paths crossed.

"Are you a sorcerer?" asked the man with a braid. He was shirtless in spite of the chill. His bronze chest was pimpled with gooseflesh. His eyes were on the wand, which emitted a wan light, casting a halo around the holder.

"Perhaps," the wand-holder replied. "Are you interested in spell craft?"

"Among other things," said the other, and suggestively stroked his crotch. And so, under the spangletrees, they shared and spilled seed by coaxing and cajoling, pulling and pushing, biting and spitting, among other things.

After the unsavory business concluded, they parted ways under cover of the sparkling mist, both of them spattered with spangles of all kinds. This was when the magician saw that he no longer had the wand.

A magician without a wand is like an eunuch.

Magic collects in the body with no means of escape. It flows through the body's systems, wreaking havoc. Oozes out of pores, corroding and transforming. The magician could feel the magic in his veins, thrumming with strange music. His right kidney became an ear, and he could hear the swoosh and swirl of bodily functions. Some other minor organ, maybe his appendix, began speaking in some hoarse language. Had it grown a mouth? He'd heard of such things. The tide of enchantment dribbled out in his body fluids. Urine changed to every color in spectrum and his sweat became iridescent bubbles. His body sprouted a single breast. Worst of all, his skin began to change. It blistered and peeled. The features beneath the skin had been recast. They were the green of chalcedony. When this happened, he know that he didn't have long.

Shaangö was a small isle, and the town abutting the spangletree grove was tiny. Less than a week passed when the magician began hearing whispers about a madman in the town square with long black braided hair.

As he approached the square, the magician saw people moving away, gossiping and giggling about the mad fool. Over the din of the market place, he heard a hoarse voice, croaking out nihilistic nonsense.

The magician found the thief in the square's fountain, splashing around and conversing with the stone cherubs who spat out water between their lips. He held the wand in one hand. It was necrotic green. His skin on his chest had blistered, revealing a twisted star the same color as the wand, and the magician's face.

The organ in the magician's body began shrieking; he could hear it echoing in his bones.

In one quick bound, he was in the filthy water, along with the thief, who, in his magic-induced madness, was no longer quite so comely. He snatched the wand back, and yanked the thief's braid.

"Fool," the magician said, "You have doomed us both!"

Even as he spoke, more blotches of that awful green bloomed on both their bodies.

7'0"
6'6"
6'0"
5'6"
5'0"
4'6"
4'0"
3'6"
EDWARD LEE
THE STATEMENT OF
SGT JUSTIN JESSOP
OF THE INNMOUTH
POLICE DEPARTMENT

OFFICER: EDWARD LEE

SUBJECT: THE STATEMENT OF SGT. JUSTIN JESSOP

DATE: 04/20/2020

INTERVIEWER: When did you realize that something was seriously wrong?

JESSOP: Yesterday morning about 8 a.m. I was in the patrol car, so the chief radioed me and said that Hanna Tilton just called, said a man with no legs was dragging himself across the New Church Green. We both kind of laughed at that, 'cos Hanna Tilton's about ninety and nuttier than a truckload of fruitcakes. Hell, last Christmas she called and said Santa Claus had come down her chimney-with his dick out, and Hanna doesn't even have a chimney. Anyway, I had to check it out, so I drove the car over and...and—

INTERVIEWER: What did you find?

JESSOP (sighs): I found Matt Eliot dragging himself across the Green with no legs. I got out and tried to help him but there wasn't anything I could do. His legs looked ripped out of his hip sockets, no stumps to get tourniquets on. Whoever did it also pulled his cock and balls off and put it in his shirt pocket. No lie. What kind of lunatic would do something like that? Anyway, right before he died he said, "Tis all true, Justin. The stories from the old days. Them things started comin' ashore from the reef about sun up, bust right into the plant where we was all workin'-"

INTERVIEWER: The plant? Can you specify?

JESSOP: On Water Street. Matt works in one of the fish-packing plants there...or I should say worked. "They kicked all the loading doors down," he said. "Barged right in and start killin' everyone, pullin' off heads, yankin' out guts. Throwed Ezra Dunning, the floor super, right smack dab into the chum-maker. And any women workin' the gutting line--well, those things got right to it, fuckin' them gals every which way while's they was screamin' to high heaven. The prettier ones, like Marsha Cobb'n Belinda Bishop-they carried 'em off, and the old ones'n not so good lookin' ones, shit, they fed 'em right through the big band saw we use to cut up the tunas. Ya could tell by lookin' at 'em-they was doin' it just fer fun..." That's when Matt bled out, so first thing I did was get on the radio but before I could call for backup, Chief Dodgeson was on the line, screaming: "Jessop! Get out'a town! These things come up Madison street

STATION:INNSMOUTH POLICE DEPARTMENT

OFFICER: EDWARD LEE

SUBJECT: THE STATEMENT OF SGT. JUSTIN JESSOP

DATE: 04/20/2020

and are all over the place, killin' everybody!" and then came some gunshots, some grisly tearing sounds and-that was the last I heard from the chief.

INTERVIEWER: So, what were the "things?" Did you see them your-self?

JESSOP: "For shit's sake! Of course I saw 'em, then, and after they died! You're telling me that you didn't see the bodies?

INTERVIEWER: This isn't about what I saw, sergeant. Let's keep this interview objective. It's about what you saw.

JESSOP: Well, fuck, okay. The things mostly looked like what the old Innsmouth legends say: big watery eyes that never blink; long, thin-lipped mouths; creases of skin on the sides of their necks that look like they might be gills. Bunch of fucked-up deformities all mixed up to one degree or another with human aspects.

INTERVIEWER: Would you describe the non-human traits as ich-thyic or batrachian?

JESSOP: The fuck? What's that mean?

INTERVIEWER: Fish-like, frog-like, that sort of thing?

JESSOP: Yes, yes-whatever! Worse than that! Most of 'em had fully changed over-you know, like the legend says, and some of 'em-fuck!-they must've been the full-blooded ones, like the old stories talk about. Then I drove down past the fire sta-tion-jeez! The fuckin' place was on fire! And there was some-thing wrong with the radio-I couldn't get through anywhere, not even on the state band. Cellphone wouldn't work either, almost like those things had some way to jam it. So then I tear-ass over to the Holiday Inn Express that used to be the old Gilman House Hotel, thought I could use their landline but, fuck... First thing I see when I went in was three of these things all fuckin' the front desk

STATION:INNSMOUTH POLICE DEPARTMENT

OFFICER: EDWARD LEE

SUBJECT: THE STATEMENT OF SGT. JUSTIN JESSOP

DATE: 04/20/2020

And don't ask me to describe the dicks on these things stop and start to come after me, so I dropped the lot of 'em with four single head-shots. I notice through the front window that a bunch of others already had my patrol car tipped over and were setting it on fire, and the worst part was they tipped it over deliberate on Brandy Babcock from the bakery, who was eight months pregnant, and then I see more of 'em pourin' into the town square and coming out of the rec center that they say used to be that weirdo church, Something-or-other Order of the Dragon or Dagon or something like that. I just said fuck it and ran out the hotel's back door. Even with all the screaming coming from the rooms, there wasn't anything I could do. I hauled ass across Lafayette Street, cut through the old Marsh lot where that mansion used to be, then found myself in the back way of the old closed church on Adam's Lane. I jimmied my way in and finally found the stairs to the bell tower, so that's where I went, right up those stairs into the tower. I peeked down from the tower, took one look toward the docks, and passed out.

INTERVIEWER: What did you see?

JESSOP: What do ya think? More of those things, but not hundreds of 'em, thousands of 'em, thousands of those, of those monsters. When I saw all that, I guess I went into shock and lost consciousness. Didn't wake up again for almost twenty-four hours, and that's when I came down 'cos I saw the military vehicles and all those front loaders shoveling up all the bodies of those things.

INTERVIEWER: You're a very lucky man, Sergeant Jessop. Only a few other townspeople survived.

JESSOP: Well...how did you kill them all like that? At first I thought it might be something like nerves gas or something, but then I would've died too, right?

INTERVIEWER: It wasn't us, sergeant. You really want to know what killed all those things? Well, I'll tell you. It was the fucking coronavirus...

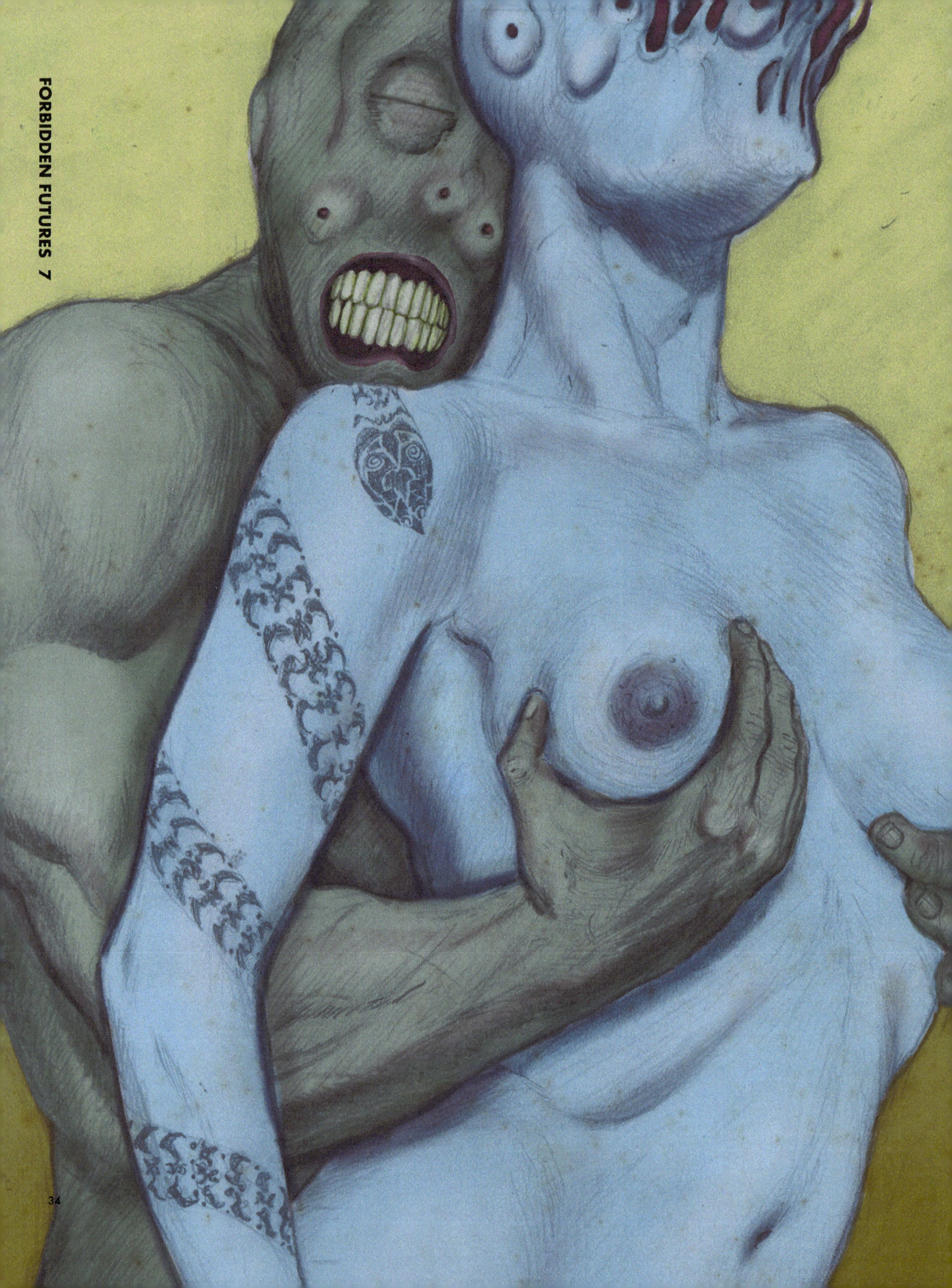

MOTHER'S MARK BY BRENDAN VIDITO

In the middle of the night, the fissure on her apartment wall bulged and disgorged a man encased in an amniotic sheath. He struck the decaying floorboards with a pulpy crack, white fluid pooling around his huddled form. The woman crouching in the corner of the room—impatient for this moment—stood up and approached him. The sensory organs on her face danced in response to this new and intriguing stimulus. Already, she could feel herself growing wet with desire. Hopefully her latest experiment would yield positive results.

Rolling up the sleeves of her satin robe, she used one fingernail to slice an opening in the amniotic sac. Clear liquid gushed out, washing over the ruptured sheath and diluting the white substance already spread across the floor. The woman reached inside. Nutrient sacs and capillaries tangled in her fingers as she probed for the man's forearm, gripped it, and pulled. The Mother's Mark, wrapped like a living tattoo around her upper arm and shoulder, glowed a faint orange in the gloom. Its blessing coursed through her muscle fibers, imbuing her with the strength necessary to lift the man to his feet and hold him in a clumsy standing position. His legs were unsteady, their musculature hardening and springing into shape as she watched.

He was a handsome specimen, two fingers above six feet and broad in the shoulders. His body and head were devoid of hair or follicles. His mouth was lipless and filled with long, narrow teeth designed for sexual biting. The woman had also outfitted his skull with biological accessories intended to enhance pleasure: lubricating orifices, an organic vibrating module, and pores that excreted a sensation heightening gel. The woman held his shoulders, looked up into his face. He certainly looked better than her previous efforts, but the true test lay in his functionality and abilities.

She glanced around the room to ensure she was alone. It was cluttered with broken and dirty laboratory equipment. The apartment's electricity was being funneled into a massive chest freezer that hummed like something alive. Inside were the pieces of organic matter she intended to recycle from failed experiments—she had eaten the rest, roasting the flesh over a propane stove. The four corners of the bachelor were occupied by birthing nodules the woman had recovered from the street, where they had fallen from the sky bound body of the Great Mother. They had long since metastasized into the building itself, allowing her experiments to transition from wet dream to reality.

Her senses honed on the single blacked-out window. Beyond was the city with its rivers of flesh and the Great Mother watching from above. As always, the woman would have to ensure her experiments remained a secret. The Great Mother had eradicated the male species for a reason, and any attempt to reconstruct or resurrect their kind was punishable by death.

She passed a hand over the man's face, her sensory organs droning a reverse lullaby. The man shuddered violently, breath surging into his body. Mere seconds elapsed as he acclimated to his environment, and then he was upon her, grasping her waist with sinewy hands, and pressing his mouth against her neck. The woman moaned softly, curling her fingers around his biceps, and tilting her head back to encourage his advances. His teeth pinched her flesh and pulled, sending a white-hot streak of pain through her nerve-endings. A little too hard, she noted, but that could easily be adjusted. Then he spun her around, tearing the robe away in a flash of gleaming crimson, and squeezed her breasts. Hot, pheromone-laced breath panted against her neck. His cock, eight inches long and studded with fat deposits to increase pleasure, rubbed against the cleft of her ass. She tried to loosen his grip on her, but he only tightened his hold so she could barely move. Memories of past, failed experiments flooded her mind. Not again, she thought. Why couldn't she breed the primal aggression from her subjects? Was it so firmly rooted in their sexual identities? Not for the first time, the woman wondered if this violence was the reason the Great Mother had purged them from existence.

The Mother's Mark flared a bright orange. The woman effortlessly pulled herself away from the man. Spun around. Gripped the sides of his head. And decapitated him with a casual upward motion of her hands. Blood pumped from the ragged hole in his neck, and his body collapsed, twitching, to the floor. She tossed the head into a corner of her room and looked down. A thick stream of seminal fluid trailed away from his softening erection. The woman hummed disappointment. Another failure, but at least she would have something to eat tonight.

THE KING-HOLE CHRONICLES VOL. 8 INSTALLMENT 2: THE NEW KING

MATTHEW BARTLETT

IN THE PREVIOUS INSTALLMENT:

King Fgggg lay sprawled on the onyx tiled floor, his life's blood leaping in fountains that painted the walls, slaughtered by contract by his own guards in exchange for six full bottles of IE9DD6, the newest strain, whose potency had been tested, with spectacular results, by the Glapttz Syndicate, who had finally wearied of the king's strident and unyielding efforts, backed by his shadow-army, to dissolve their outfit. Syndicate proxies had contacted the guards with the offer. Six bottles could last the two guards fourteen lifetimes, but greed and proportionality were strangers to the duo as, incidentally, were hygiene and integrity. As the King bled out onto the floor, cursing them; berating them; begging them; complimenting them effusively; promising them even more IE9DD6, which he couldn't possibly get his seven hands on; and then cursing them again, they flogged their fat, floppy thorns enthusiastically,, finally spewing steaming streams of turbid sputum into Fgggg's eyes. His shrieks, shrill and loud, followed them down the path to the pub..

The Council of Adamants held an emergency meeting in the Seventh Cave of Crowns. A new king would have to be formulated. It had been forty-five years, more than double the lifetime of the eldest council member, but the formulae carved into the cave wall was still legible, and the apparatus, though bile-strewn and bruised, was still very much operational.

In the ensuing squabble to select the selectors of the king-makers, four of the Council were killed and one decapitated, sent home with his weeping head tucked into his belt. The meeting was considered a success, and the two chosen selectors of the king-makers, Leland Van Ian and Kyrkun, conferred briefly in the light allowed in by the King-Hole, also referred to as the Smoke-Hole, then set out to find their pair.

INSTALLMENT 2: THE NEW KING

THE SATURNINE CLOUDS of orange and periwinkle began to hiss as they bumble-tumbled through the mottled sky, turning it over onto its spagellated back, causing it to spill its colors into the Farkahoryt Sea. The peaks and plateaus expanded and flushed red, having pulled in blood-air from the undersurface. The roar of the Kenker subsided. The ferferts started up their song right where they had left off.

It was night.

ANOTHER NEW PLANET on which to fuck. What was this, their twentieth? Twenty-first? The air of unpredictability, the risk, the promise of the unexpected and the unknown—it all turned Goirg38 on. Amaaak7 too, though she'd never tell him that.

They had positioned themselves on a quite agreeable sand-topped plateau across a dust-bush-riddled valley from a strange mountain with some sort of spout jutting like a swollen, truncated thumb from one of its narrower peaks.

No matter the planet, Amaaak7 was eloquent in her agonies, and given to clawing at his paws, which irritated Goirg38 and prolonged his exertions, which hurt her further. Goirg38's pricks were barbed, the exquisite pain they inflicted exacerbated by their swelling and their fusing, the resulting blood both a lubricant and an irritant. The chains had been his idea, the only way to stop her reflexive scratching. The insults he could stand, but the injuries were a bridge too far.

Now, though, her paws shook, causing the chains to rattle, and her insults flowed faster and more inventive, jumbling Goirg38's concentration, dampening his lusts just slightly. This was preferable to torn-up paws. How much easier it would have been for her to just agree to clip her nails. He came desultorily and flung himself to the ground in a pout. Before long, he fell away into an agreeable oblivion.

AMAAAK7 SLIPPED her paws from the chains. The weird protuberance on the mountain across the valley was uttering strange sounds again, mingling with Goirg38's snores to create a jarring duet. Goirg38, curled up on his side in a drying pool of bloodied semen, slept right through the din. He'd never hear it, anyway. Goirgs' inner ears were notoriously wadded and crumpled, permitting only certain sounds in. Amaaak7 stood and stretched. She squatted and spewed out a hundred wriggling green things that slithered away in search of food. That done, she too could sleep, the cacophony notwithstanding. She lay with her lower back pressed against his. Hunger gripped her. There was nothing to eat here.

THE DYING KING woke at dawn, weeping and trembling. He was on his back on a cold and hard but wet surface. Before his eyes was only blackness in which amorphous blobs of color changed shape, fusing and billowing, coming apart and rejoining in new and uninteresting shapes. His back ached and his body screamed. He screamed as well, the screams resolving into words, pleas for them to finish him, to put an end to his agonies. The further he climbed into wakefulness, the more the pain seared him inside and out. Somewhere in his crazed mind he knew they would not let him die until a new king was created. He also knew that the process took a bit of time. He fell mercifully away, then almost instantly awoke again for another bout of screaming. Oh, how it hurt.

"THEM," SAID Leland Van Ian.

"Which?" replied Kyrkun.

"Them alien ones."

Kyrkun grabbled the quatronoculars and peered into them. A male cat-like creature, broad of snout and fluffy-tailed with wee spiraling horns and long ears, and a buxom female of the same species, smaller, with delicate features and very sharp fangs. Both had legs like the trunks of bhaddo trees. "The one with the ears and the one with the teats?"

"Them."

"Why would you pick alien ones?"

"I dunno. Something different."

"The Council of Adamants selected us to do this. And you want to take a chance like that? Go out on a limb? They'll kill us."

"If they selected us...that means what?"

Kyrkun tilted his head and his eyes went funny.

Van Ian sighed. "It means the Council trusts our judgement."

"And after this, it won't."

"It's these two who shall make the new King," said Van Ian in a tone of finality. "Definitely them. All they do is fuck and sleep. They're base, vacuous creatures without guile. They're perfect."

Kyrkun said, "Fine, but you tell them."

Van Ian stared him down.

Kyrkun stared back as long as he could, which wasn't long at all. "Fine," he said. "I'll do it."

THE STRANGE LITTLE being approached from the east. Starry ears, a profusion of whiskers, four eyes forming a square around a pinkish blob of a nose. Goirg38 sensed the creature, sensed there was to be a request, a proposal of some kind, perhaps a demand backed by force. Its nature was vague but not disagreeable. Any other time he might have chewed the little fellow to shreds just to see what he tasted like, but he was in fine fettle today, well-fucked and with a belly full of goosegrass. "Well?" he said.

Kyrkun gasped. So much for the element of surprise. "Oh! Hi! Yes. Er...I have a question."

"Go ahead."

"You and the sleeping one there, you have been selected to aid in the production of our new king."

"I didn't hear a question."

Kyrkun sighed. "That smoke-hole across the way, you will...that is, will you...?"

"Get to it."

"I need you two to...will you two fuck next to it, then you have to...will you...come into it?"

"What's a smoke-hole?"

"That thing sticking out over yonder."

"I'm afraid I can't. We have to make babies every time. Every time."

Kyrkun squeezed his eyes shut, and Goirg38 felt a searing agony in his testicle-cluster. "That is one five-hundredth of the pain I can inflict," the former said.

Goirg38 shot back with "and one seven-thousandth of that which I can take."

Which turned out to be a lie.

THE VALLEY WAS BIGGER than

Amaaak7 had thought, the strange mountain farther away. She had awakened to see Goirg38 and an odd little character, who both explained to her in overlapping, confusing words about some kind of venture for which she and her mate had been recruited. The details were unimportant to her, except for the fact that there would be no offspring this time, and for those never-to-be born she mourned, and then got over it. To hell with it, it'd be a story to tell their other kazillion kids on the propitious day of their inevitable return.

The main issue now was boredom. Her mate and the recruiter were best pals now, it seemed, and they'd been joined by a third, a human grotesquerie who went by the vomitous name of Van Ian. A real boys' club, and the human was ogling her. Through the pinwheels of dustbrush they trudged, and the mountain seemed to retreat from them periodically, as though afraid.

So Goirg38 was supposed to waste his semen, shoot it down a hole, and this would somehow create a king? And he couldn't just whack off into it? No, because his barbs would hurt his precious paws. And her juices had to be involved somehow. An idea formed in her mind. She grinned. The human, Van Ian, his ogling turned to a look of concern. She adjusted her breasts, and that look went right back to lustful.

FROM THE PEAK by the smoke-hole,

looking away from the plateau and down, the sweep of the land was majestic. A city lay in the middle distance, towering edifices connected by great bridges, colored lights, strange vehicles whizzing along wire tracks. Wiry winged creatures hung in the air, gesticulating with spindly legs and pincers. Sounds carried up to them on winds fragrant with heretofore unsmelled spices: bleeps and belches and thunderclaps and babbles, chortles and weeping and wisps of curious songs. Nearby, the smoke-hole sighed and thumped, made a sound something like laughter.

"Turn your heads," said Goirg38.

"It's nothing we haven't seen before."

"I'm not a performer. I don't want an audience."

Van Ian and Krykun turned and looked back across the interminable valley they'd just traversed.

GOIRG38 UNSHEATHED HIS UNITS.

Amaaak7 raised her hips.

Nothing.

Come on, he thought. He looked down at Amaaak7, who was now cuffed and ready to receive him. He thought briefly of Amaaak6. That didn't do it. Ah, but Amaaak5. Her inner eyelids. Her spiraling stare. Her slit-thin nostrils. That did it. He slid in effortlessly. Amaaak5 cursed and gnashed. Good, good. He pumped and pumped and pumped some more. "Cover your ears," he said. The human and the weirdo covered their ears. But the human spread apart his fingers.

Goirg38 felt the pressure building. He dismounted, crouched, and shot an arc right over Amaaak7's head and into the smoke-hole. "Bullseye!" hollered the human. "It didn't even touch the sides!"

Goirg38 re-mounted Amaaak7 and the couple stayed very still. From the smoke-hole there came a great rumbling roar. Van

Ian and Kyrkun stepped as far back as possible. The ground trembled. A keening noise now, like metal on metal.

And then came the smoke. First it was a thin white vine, spiraling into the air, accompanied by a mephitic odor. The stream grew thicker, the odor more dank, and then in the white a darker grey interior manifested. The grey went green, then black, then a curious blue. It formed organs. A seven-chambered heart. A veined triad of elongated lungs. A fat brown liver. A smallish stomach, out of which grey intestines unspooled. Teeth shot out from the core and gathered, clacking without rhythm. Two bulging, black-veined eyes popped out from top of the column, unseeing, then seeing, then full of fear, then madness, then betraying a stark idiocy. Two smoky arms drooled out from the midsection. The whole thing began to go liquidy, then coalesce into a solid. A thin, papery skin formed. Van Ian clutched his midsection and vomited into the sand. Kyrkun laughed maniacally, pulled out a thin violet pecker, and began pumping it with his fists.

Goirg38 pulled, and then passed, out.

Amaaak7 ignored the pain. She waited.

A mouth opened in the nascent face. "Gurf," it said. "Gurffa gak frunkle…aaaAAAAAAAAA" and the scream rose in pitch and timbre and volume until it was a siren-like shriek. Kyrkun's eardrums burst and his lobes went black. Van Ian went to his knees, his hands over his ears. Goirg38 twitched in his sleep, eyelids fluttering, lip curling, revealing a bone-white fang.

Amaaak7 made her move. She leapt, catching the fragile new king against her chest, her strong front legs encircling its torso. The king's ankles shattered, leaving two malformed feet, still mostly just smoke and toenails, jammed partly into the aperture of the smoke hole. Blood welled up. Amaaak7 and the nascent king sailed out into the air over the canyon and plummeted. As they fell, Amaak7 dug her teeth into the king's throat, sucking and slurping at the blood. The king gasped and batted uselessly at her sides with arms supported by bones as thin as the pinbones of a grantlefish.

Up by the smoke-hole, Van Ian leapt forward, pulling from his waistband a long-barreled pistol. He shot at the descending pair. The flaming bolts missed, all of them, every single one, flaring out and dissolving just shy of their target. Defeated, he put the pistol's barrel under his chin and shot. Flaming brains shot outward in every direction.

Amaaak7 landed on her feet. She devoured the new king. It whispered as it went back into oblivion. It had words now, and those words could just be heard over the chewing. Amaak7 listened. It was poetry.

Pure poetry.

She finished him.

IN NEXT WEEK'S INSTALLMENT:

Vol. 8 Installment 3—The Smoke-Hole Afterbirth: Amaaak7 and Goirg38 split up on a temporary basis. Kyrkun has his hearing with the Council of Adamants. The dying king's agonies intensify. Disquiet in the Glapttz Syndicate leads to all-out civil war. The author ingests a heroic does of IE9DD6. The Seventh Cave of Crowns is vandalized, and EOIRf8u suspects his very daughter as the culprit. Margaret Van Ian and her team of intrepid investigators arrive from Earth in search of her husband. The smoke-hole ejects something foul. It makes its slimy way toward the city. There is a sparsely attended funeral at which occurs violence and coprophagy and endocannibalism. But exactly whose funeral?

Tune in, won't you?

PLASTER CASTER

BY KIM VODICKA

You approached me as I slept and, taking care not to look directly at me, but guided by my image reflected in the black mirror you bore, slashed my throat ear to ear and cut off my head with a hunting knife. Now I am your spirit wife. Now I have died and become a myth. If the ass is a hole that sucks, the neck is a hole that resists. The real question is how to stick it in without having to behold my frightening countenance. The black mirror is the answer. Prop it up on a stump and livestream the action. We're in the woods, of course, where all the best bad things happen.

The black mirror displays my head in your hands. You point the severed part toward the camera, to get a sense of things. You'll have two holes to choose from. You decide to try the windpipe first. It's a bit of a stab in the dark, as there's only so much you can see in 2D. My windpipe doesn't seem to want to suck you in. The only thing keeping you from losing your erection is anger, secondary only to the thrill of total possession via annihilation. You fuck it with a few stern thrusts, ripping through vein, cartilage, and muscle, squeezing my neck to let blood and ease entry, almost as basic and boring as fucking the cunt of a consenting human being. You lose your erection but not the will to make me yours completely.

Total possession necessitates blowing loads into the dead, or the severed heads of the world's most horrifying women. Maybe my upper esophageal sphincter will do better. You point the severed part of my head toward the camera, to reassess things. When face-up, the upper esophageal sphincter sits just below the trachea, the way an asshole sits just below a cunt hole in missionary. You squeeze my neck to let more blood. It's still warm. You'd think the blood of a reptilian gorgon would be cold, but you learn something new with each corpse. You stick it in. At first, it's mostly resistance, but once you get beyond the tip, it sucks you right in, the way an asshole reluctantly, inevitably receives a dick. Now you're really getting somewhere.

As you dissociate into the pleasure of the moment, you feel a slithering between your upper thighs. The slithering tickles your scrotum, now flush with the severed portions of my skin and flesh. My hair tentacles still have some life in them. Reptilian bodies tend to go on a bit longer because they're more efficient. They don't need as much oxygen. They tickle your scrotum and perineum in the way known only to the lips and tongues and fingertips of the world's most horrifying women, the world's greatest dick suckers. You welcome their pleasure and bray—half-man, half-ass, all beast. A lone tentacle creeps just past the point of welcoming, rimming your asshole with its forked tongue, licking clean the stalactites. The pleasure blinds. As it slithers into your asshole, in a slinky though steady trajectory, you see nothing but the bright white light paramount to transcendence. As my many other hair tentacles wrap around your hips and ass, tethering you to my neck hole, all is binding.

It's just so god damn funny, I can't help but let out a laugh. It isn't the laugh of duping subservience. The laugh of the medusa is the laugh of the abyss. When you fuck it, it fucks you back. I choke-chortle on your cock and my own blood. The load you mean to blow in me is nigh. I feel it coming on. Rigor mortis, that is. You thought the head of the medusa would be immune to such things, but she's human. She, too, can freeze.

Your dick gets stuck. The blinding light of transcendence quickly turns into the dull haze of panic. You could've fucked my neck holes face-down, but the danger excited you. In the theater of corpse fucking, risk takes all. As you frantically try to dislodge your cock from my neck hole, you forget the danger of looking into my frightening countenance, known to freeze and fix into place even the noblest of knights and most savage of tenants, and my wild dead eyes meet yours.

Your dick turns to stone, of course, never mind the rest of you. My head falls to the ground with a thoughtless thud. I cough-chortle your petrified cock out of my neck hole. It takes on a look of chaste austerity, of sudden admiration and blank awe. The black mirror saw it all. Someone will be around to collect my head, eventually. Maybe they'll put it in a museum, immortalize it as an artifact of a tired, deadly myth made legend.

Whatever becomes of me, I am your spirit wife, but you're still with me.

THE IMP AND THE SMOKE ANGEL
BY ED KURTZ

"Ah, fuck," Matik says, narrowing his tremendous blackglass eyes to slits at the figure approaching in the middle-distance. "It's Urdok."

Matik stops grinding with the quern between his knees and throws a glance back at his mate, Forra. Her massive ears flatten against the sides of her smooth, hairless head as she wipes her hands on her apron, leaving broad smears of dark blood from the fowl she has just slaughtered in the dooryard.

"What the hell is he dragging, the fool?" she asks Matik.

"Fucking lunatic," Matik growls. "I do believe he's stark naked."

"You mean naked?"

"I mean I can see his cock."

Forra shakes her head and, by proxy, her ears in disgust. Urdok has never been anything but trouble, though his leaving the village two seasons hence was a blessing upon which everyone could agree. And yet, here the son of a bitch came, back home, nude as a skinfox and dragging what appeared to Forra to be a massive stone on a crudely-made travois. And is he singing?

Forra makes a sound in the pit of her throat and hurries back into the cottage. She's seen enough.

Matik, on the other hand, sets the quern down on the ground beside his stool, done with grinding grains for the time being. A more pressing issue has been presented to him.

"Urdok? Is that you?"

"Surprised?" the giddy imp calls back. "Thought I died, yes? No, Matik, no. Not dead. Not Urdok."

"Here," Matik says, rising from his stool and stepping down into the road. "Let me help you."

He can all but feel his wife's displeasure with him from inside the cottage, but Matik was never one to refuse an imp a helping hand—even one as guileful, and nude, as Urdok. Though, were he to be completely honest with himself, what Matik would really like most right now is a closer look at the imp's strange, heavy freight. "Say, what is this all about, Urdok?"

The prodigal imp stops in his tracks as Matik meets him in the road and, wiping his brow with the back of his hand, he says, "Power."

With this, he titters. His tail swipes the dust in the road and the stone seems to tremble on the travois. Matik averts his gaze from Urdok and, at last, takes in the stone Urdok has dragged for who-knows-how-many kilometers from who-knows-where. It is porous like sandstone, wet and glimmering in the midday light knifing through the treetops. He starts to look back when it seems to him that some of the tiny holes in the surface of the rock are almost imperceptibly opening and closing. Like gills.

Matik looks again, more closely. Urdok continues to giggle, both tail and cock wobbling rudely. This is when, in the dead center of the huge, lumpy stone, a massive eye opens and trains its gleaming pupil directly at Matik.

"Fuck!" Matik cries, staggering backward, away from it.

Urdok shrieks, "Don't mind if I do!" And no sooner does Matik fall back onto his ass than Urdok is up and over the top of the stone, maneuvering his rapidly stiffening member into the nearest of the opening and constricting orifices. The humongous black eye does not alter course. It keeps staring directly at Matik whilst Urdok humps the stone's surface, off to the left of it.

"Horrible, horrible," Matik mutters, but naturally, he cannot keep his eyes away from the whole spectacle. Nor does he so much as blink when a dozen or so of the holes Urdok isn't violating erupt with quivering tendrils that writhe their way up and out into the open air like corpseworms sated from their nocturnal feasts. The tendrils seem to grow in length and girth, whipping at the air around the eye, around Urdok, though neither are deterred. The eye stares at Matik. Urdok fucks the rock. The tendrils wriggle madly.

And then, the smoke comes. Smoke that billows white and thick into the shape of a woman hovering overhead.

A human woman.

With wings like a snowgrackle.

"Do you see, Matik?" Urdok squeals. "Do you see?"

He sees. He can't stop seeing. The winged woman, half-smoke and half-real, unfolds herself and smiles broadly at the grotesque tableau beneath her.

"I found this," says Urdok. "It's mine. Mine. It's mine, damn you all."

He shivers and stiffens, presumably ejaculates inside of the rock he has dragged down the road from the world beyond, and the smoke angel regards him warmly, motherly, her pale face pink at the cheeks and eyes glinting with kindness, before she descends upon Urdok and begins to feed.

The imp's bones splinter. His flesh tears and blood flows darkly. He does not resist, and what Matik at first thinks is a scream he later reinterprets as a cry of ecstasy.

Matik scrabbles away, finds his feet, bolts back into the cottage and bars the door. At dusk, he dares to peek. The stone is gone. The travois, too. No Urdok and no smoke angel. Not even a drop of blood.

He releases a long, slow breath and thinks, I have to find it.

CREDITS

MICHAEL ALLEN ROSE is a writer, musician and performer based in Chicago, IL. He makes music under the name Flood Damage, and has published several books with various small presses. He likes cats and good tea. You can find out more at www.gerbilprobe.com

GREGORY NORMAN BOSSERT is an author, filmmaker, and musician, based in the San Francisco Bay Area. He started writing on a dare in 2009 at the age of 47, and has no intention of stopping. His story "The Telling" won the 2013 World Fantasy Award. When not writing, he wrangles spaceships and superheroes for legendary visual effects studio Industrial Light & Magic. More information is available at GregoryNormanBossert.com.

EDWARD LEE is an American novelist specializing in the field of horror, and has authored 40 books, more than half of which have been published by mass-market New York paperback companies such as Leisure/Dorchester, Berkley, and Zebra/Kensington. He is a Bram Stoker award nominee for his story "Mr. Torso," and his short stories have appeared in over a dozen mass-market anthologies, including THE BEST AMERICAN MYSTERY STORIES OF 2000, Pocket's HOT BLOOD series, and the award-wining 999. Several of his novels have sold translation rights to Germany, Greece, and Romania. He also publishes quite actively in the small-press/limited-edition hardcover market.

JEFF STRAND is a four-time nominee (and zero-time winner, but c'mon, he lost to Stephen King TWICE!) of the Bram Stoker Award. He is a two-time nominee and one-time WINNER!!!! of the Splatterpunk Award. His novels are usually classified as horror, but they're really all over the place, almost always with a great big dose of humor. He's written five young adult novels that all fall into the "really goofy comedy" category. His book STALKING YOU NOW was adapted into the feature film MINDY HAS TO DIE, which premiered at the Yellow Fever Independent Film Festival in Belfast, Ireland. He lives in Atlanta, Georgia with his wife and one gigantic freaking cat.

BRENDAN VIDITO is the author of the Wonderland Award-winning collection of body horror stories, Nightmares in Ecstasy (Clash Books, 2018). His work has appeared in several anthologies and magazines. He also co-edited The New Flesh: A Literary Tribute to David Cronenberg (Weirdpunk Books, 2019) with Sam Richard. You can visit him at brendanvidito.com or follow him on social media.

KIM VODICKA is the author of three full-length poetry collections—Aesthesia Balderdash (Trembling Pillow Press, 2012), Psychic Privates (White Stag Publishing, 2018), and The Elvis Machine (CLASH Books, 2020). She is also the creator of a poetic comic book series, a chapbook of sound poems on vinyl, and an illustrated book of poetry. Her poems, art, and essays have been featured in Spork, Queen Mob's Teahouse, Paper Darts, Best American Experimental Writing, Luna Magazine, Really Serious Literature, The Thought Erotic, Nasty! and many others. For the past decade, she has toured the country performing spoken word with musical accompaniment. Originally from south Louisiana, she lives in Memphis, Tennessee with her beloved cat, Lula. Cruise her at www.kimvodicka.com

ED KURTZ is the author of A Wind of Knives, Bleed, Nausea, The Rib from Which I Remake the World, and other novels and novellas. Ed's short fiction has been honored in both Best American Mystery Stories, and Best Gay Stories. He lives in New England with author Doungai Gam.

CAROLYN WATSON DUBISCH is an artist, illustrator, sculptor and author. In her years as a professional artist she's created giant vegetables for a Washington DC Museum, helped create two dozen tiny hot air balloons for a Vegas show and designed alien bird-men for Star Wars games.

CRAIG LAURANCE GIDNEY writes both contemporary and genre fiction in his native Washington, D.C. He is the author of the collections *Sea, Swallow Me & Other Stories* (Lethe Press, 2008), *Bereft* (Tiny Satchel Press, 2013), *Skin Deep Magic* (Rebel Satori Press, 2014), *The Nectar of Nightmares* (Dim Shores, 2015) and *A Spectral Hue* (Word Horde, 2019).

CODY GOODFELLOW has written eight novels. His latest are UNAMERICA (King Shot Press) and SCUM OF THE EARTH (Eraserhead Press). His first two collections, SILENT WEAPONS FOR QUIET WARS and ALL-MONSTER ACTION, received the Wonderland Book Award. As an actor, he has appeared in numerous short films, TV shows, music videos and commercials. He "lives" in Portland, OR.

MIKE DUBISCH began his lifetime career in illustration and comics while still in high school, coloring comics for every major studio while writing and publishing his own short graphic works for publication. The artist never stopped exploring the subjects he enjoyed in these young years- Fantastic worlds and bizarre creatures, dynamic warriors and exotic females- and has since contributed to the worlds of Star Wars, Dungeons and Dragons, and Aliens VS Predator. Working with author Tom Simmons, Mike is in the final stages of adapting a long out of print Edgar Rice Burroughs novel in web comic form. His work in films and book illustration is well known by fans of the Cthulhu Mythos of H.P. Lovecraft. Lately Mike has concentrated on exploring his personal obsessions and traveling the world on location sketching in Morocco, Mexico, Latin America and the UK, while teaching online at the Academy Of University in San Francisco. See more at MikeDubisch.com